THE USBORNE BOOK OF

BIRD FACTS

Bridget Gibbs

CONTENTS

Illustrated by Tony Gibson and Stephen Lings

Designed by Tony Gibson

**Consultant: Rob Hume,
Editor of *BIRDS* magazine, published by
The Royal Society for the Protection of Birds**

What is a bird?

How many birds?

There are about 8,600 different kinds, or species, of birds in the world. These are split into 28 groups called orders. More than half of all living birds are in the songbirds group.

Marathon fliers

Many birds can quickly travel vast distances to take advantage of the seasons and the best supplies of food. This movement is called migration. The champion migrant is the Arctic tern. It covers a round trip of 40,000km (25,000 miles) from the Arctic to the Antarctic and back. Terns can live for more than 20 years.

Featuring feathers

Birds are the only animals with feathers. When you look at a perched bird, most of the feathers you see are small ones that give its body a warm, smooth covering. When flying, birds show the larger, stiffer wing feathers used for flight.

DID YOU KNOW?

Wheatears living in Greenland are larger than those found further south. Being larger helps the birds to survive cold and longer migration flights to central Africa. The farther north a bird lives, the larger it tends to be.

Waterproof birds

Ducks, swans and most sea birds spend months on water and many birds dive underwater in search of food, but they never get wet through to the skin. They coat their feathers with oil from a special gland and constantly preen to keep feathers overlapping like tiles on a roof.

Running scared

Some birds run rather than fly from danger. The wild turkey, hoopoe lark and red-legged partridge all fly quite well, but prefer to sprint short distances to get away from people or predators.

Lightest and least

Birds are the only animals with hollow bones. This makes their skeletons the lightest for their size of any animal. They have fewer bones than mammals, but they have more neck bones. Nearly all mammals, even giraffes, have seven bones in their necks. Herons have about 16 and swans have as many as 25.

Features of birds

All birds have:
Feathers
Wings (though a few, such as ostriches, cannot fly)
Hollow bones (except for some flightless and diving birds)
Beaks
All birds lay eggs

The orders* of living birds

Runners and walkers	Number of species
Ostrich	1
Rheas	2
Cassowaries, emus	4
Kiwis	5
Fliers	
Tinamous	about 50
Penguins**	18
Divers	4
Grebes	about 20
Albatrosses, petrels	90
Pelicans, gannets, cormorants	about 59
Herons, storks, ibises, flamingos	118
Ducks, geese, swans	149
Vultures, hawks, eagles, falcons	287
Pheasants, grouse, megapodes	about 265
Cranes, rails, bustards	176
Oystercatchers, plovers, sandpipers, gulls, terns	320
Pigeons	271
Cockatoos, parrots	330
Cuckoos	128
Turacos	22
Owls	146
Nightjars	95
Swifts, hummingbirds	about 400
Mousebirds	6
Trogons	about 35
Kingfishers, bee-eaters, hoopoes	196
Woodpeckers, toucans, barbets	about 400
Songbirds and perching birds (from warblers to crows)	4,800

*An order is a group. (See top of previous page.)
**Penguins have become flightless. They use their wings to swim.

Birds of the past

The bird pioneer

The earliest known bird-like creature is Archaeopteryx, which lived about 150 million years ago. Fossils show that it had feathers, a wishbone and wings like a bird, but that it also had teeth, claws on its wings and a long, bony tail like a reptile.

What a water carrier

Ancient shells of elephant bird eggs were at one time used to carry water by people in Madagascar. The giant, emu-like bird produced the largest eggs ever known, equivalent in size to 180 hen's eggs.

Dinosaur descendants?

The existence of Archaeopteryx and other creatures, with their combination of bird and reptile features, has shown that birds may be the living descendants of dinosaurs.

The largest bird ever to fly was *Argentavis magnificens* with a vast, 7.6m (25ft) wingspan. It probably did not flap its wings to fly but soared like a glider, much as South American condors do today.

Where eagles dared

The Haast eagle of New Zealand was a giant eagle with a wingspan of up to 3m (10ft). It preyed on other giants, the flightless moas. The biggest of these stood about 3m (10ft) high. The last Haast eagle died more than 500 years ago, but there may still have been some moas living in the 1800s.

Bird heavyweight

The heaviest bird of all time was *Dromornis stirtoni*. It weighed an amazing 500kg (over half a ton). This is nearly four times heavier than an ostrich, which is the largest living bird. It lived in Australia about 10 million years ago, but survived until about 25,000 years ago. Not surprisingly, Dromornis was a flightless bird.

The dawning of birds

Some of the earliest true birds were sea birds. One of these, Hesperornis, was nearly 2m (6ft) long. Its wings seem to have been almost non-existent, but its very strong legs must have made it a powerful swimmer. Unlike modern birds it had teeth.

DID YOU KNOW?

The passenger pigeon made the most rapid disappearance ever known. In the 1800s it was so common in the USA that flocks of over 2,000 million birds were estimated. By 1900 there were none left in the wild, and the last one died in a zoo in 1914.

Too tasty by half

The great auk was a big sea bird with tiny wings and quite incapable of flight. Sadly, man's greed caused it to become extinct by 1844. Both its single egg and its flesh were regarded as excellent food. Its oil was used as lamp fuel and even its feathers were valued.

When early birds lived	Date lived
Archaeopteryx	150 m.y.a.
Ichthyornis (fish bird)	85 m.y.a.
Hesperornis	80 m.y.a.
Dromornis stirtoni	10-11 m.y.a.
Argentavis magnificens	5-8 m.y.a.
Aepyornis (elephant bird)	1m-1,000 y.a.

m.y.a. = million years ago

Feather care and flight

Zippy feathers

The parts of a feather (called vanes) either side of the central shaft, are kept in shape by a system of hooks. Each vane is made up of barbs. These are held together by tiny hooks. When ruffled, a feather has only to be drawn through the bird's beak to zip the barbs together again.

How many feathers?

Feathers make up about one sixth of a bird's weight. Hummingbirds have fewest feathers, some having less than 1,000. Some swans have more than 25,000. But hummingbirds have more feathers per square centimetre than swans.

Moulting

Feathers become worn with use and are usually replaced every year. In most birds, the shedding of feathers, called moulting, is gradual, so they are still able to fly reasonably well. Ducks and geese moult all their wing feathers at once in the autumn and are unable to fly for two to four weeks.

Herons have special feathers that break up into powder. They rub this into feathers that are sticky with slime from feeding on eels. The resulting sticky balls are then removed with tiny comb-like teeth on the middle claw of each foot.

Flight patterns

Birds have different ways of flying. Large birds soar in spirals, small birds often have bouncing flight, and others fly fast and straight.

Buzzard

Chaffinch

Mallard

Fastest fliers

The fastest level flight so far reliably timed is that of the eider duck at 76kph (42mph). But the peregrine, a falcon that dives on to its prey in mid-air from a great height, can reach speeds of at least 180kph (112mph) in a dive.

Featherless freeze

Penguins seem unable to move at all when they are moulting. The emperor penguin stands on the ice for three to five weeks while its old feathers fall out in big patches. During this time, it does not eat.

In 1973 a Ruppell's griffon vulture collided with an aeroplane flying at 11,270m (37,000ft) over the coast of western Africa. This is the highest altitude at which any bird has been identified. The usual height for this vulture is up to 1,500m (5,000ft).

Flying speeds
Level flight in calm air

Bewick's swan	72kph
Mallard	65kph
Pheasant	54kph
Cedar waxwing	46kph
Grey heron	43kph
Swift	40kph
Starling	35kph
House sparrow	30kph

Fishy business

Baby grebes are fed on fish, but their parents also feed them feathers from their own bodies. The feathers may prevent fish bones injuring the baby grebes' stomachs.

Drying out?

Cormorants often stand on sandbanks or breakwaters with their wings held out. They do not have completely waterproof plumage and may do this to dry out.

7

Plumage

Camouflage

The plumage of many birds blends with their background and helps to hide them from enemies.

Tawny frogmouth looks like a tree stump.

Bitterns pose like this to blend in with reeds.

Ringed plover is hard to spot on a pebbly beach.

Changing colour

Plumage may change colour from wear and tear. In autumn, the plumage of the male black lark of Asia is mottled. During the year the pale tips of the black feathers crumble away, so by spring the bird's plumage is black.

Seasonal switch

Ptarmigans live in the Arctic and on high mountains. To provide year-round camouflage, their plumage changes colour with the seasons. In spring it is mottled brown to blend with plants, in autumn it is grey to look like rocks and in winter it is white to match the snow.

Take terns

The colour of a bird's plumage can play a part in its search for food. Terns and many other fish-eating sea birds have white underparts. Unsuspecting fish cannot see them against the bright sky.

DID YOU KNOW?

The pink colouring of flamingos depends on the food they eat. In the wild, they filter shrimps and algae from water. In captivity, they are often fed on carrot juice to prevent their feathers fading to dull grey.

Noisy tails

Male snipes have a noisy way of showing a mate that they have found a nesting place. They fly over the site, then dive down with their stiff outer tail feathers spread out each side. These special feathers vibrate in the air, making a loud, whirring noise known as drumming.

Amazing But True

The highly ornamental phoenix fowl is bred for shows in Japan. Its fantastically long tail coverts* grow for about six years without a moult. The longest ever recorded were 10.59m (34.75ft), which is about as long as a bus.

Longest and shortest

The resplendent quetzal of Central America has magnificent, emerald green tail feathers. Over 60cm (24in) long, they are more than twice its body length. At the other extreme, birds such as kiwis and emus look tailless, having no special tail feathers.

Bouncing bishops

The red bishop of African plains is pale brown for most of the year. To find a mate, his plumage changes to black and red, and he fluffs out his feathers making him look like a brilliantly coloured ball. He then "bounces" over the grassland in a strange, bounding flight.

Follow their leader

Brent geese migrate in flocks from Siberia to Europe. To make sure they keep together and do not lose sight of one another, the birds have a white rump that is easily seen from behind in flight.

Tail length compared to total length

	Total length	Tail length
Crested argus pheasant	240cm	173cm
Peacock	225cm	160cm
Lady Amherst's pheasant	150cm	100cm
Pheasant	80cm	35cm
Red kite	60cm	25cm
Red-billed blue magpie	40cm	23cm
Paradise whydah	38cm	26cm
Malachite sunbird	25cm	14cm
Grey wagtail	19cm	8cm
Long-tailed tit	14cm	7.5cm

*The coverts are feathers which cover the bases of the wing and tail feathers.

Beaks and feet

Unique beak

The wrybill, a New Zealand plover, is the only bird in the world with a beak that curves sideways. It uses this odd beak to probe for insects under stones on beaches, but no-one knows why it is curved.

Upside-down feeder

The flamingo holds its unusual curved beak upside down for feeding. It sweeps it through shallow water, stirring up mud. Water is sucked into the beak and then pumped out through its sieve-like edges, leaving behind tiny shrimps and algae.

Getting a good grip

Birds never fall off branches when they go to sleep. They naturally grip any branch they land on, as their feet automatically lock into position with the toes clamped around the branch. To move, birds use their toe muscles to release their grip.

Record runner

The flightless ostrich has feet with only two toes, which are the most highly adapted for running of all birds. It can easily run at about 48kph (30mph) for 15-20 minutes, and over 70kph (43mph) in short bursts.

Types of toes

Most birds have four toes, but some have three and the ostrich has only two. Perching birds have feet to grasp branches, swimmers have webbed or lobed feet, and birds of prey have large, sharp talons.

Webbed foot
Canada goose

Sharp talons
Golden eagle

Lobed toes
Red-necked grebe

Perching foot
Greenfinch

Beak facts

Longest	Australian pelican	34-47cm
Longest for its size	Sword-billed hummingbird	10cm (Total length: 20cm)
Shortest	Glossy swiftlet	3mm
Broadest	Shoebill	about 12cm
Largest for its size	Toco toucan	23cm (Total length: 66cm)

Seed-eaters

Finches, buntings, parrots and other birds that eat seeds have stout, strong beaks, often with a hooked tip. These powerful beaks are used to open tough seed casings. Crossbills have the most extreme adaptation. They use their awkward-looking beaks to force open the cones of conifer trees.

DID YOU KNOW?

Puffins are the only birds to moult their beaks. In other birds, beaks constantly grow and wear down throughout their lives. Puffins have brightly coloured beaks for the mating season. The outer layer is then shed, leaving them with smaller, dull beaks for the rest of the year.

Lily-trotter

Jacanas have the longest toes of any bird. Those of the African jacana are up to 8cm (3in) long including the very long claws. The toes spread the bird's weight so that it can walk across floating waterweeds and lily pads in search of food without sinking.

Sensitive probes

Birds with long beaks used for probing for buried food can actually feel with their beaks. Snipes rely on their sensitive beaks when probing deep into wet mud in search of worms. Their beaks are also so flexible that the tip can be opened to grasp worms underground.

Amazing But True

Pelicans have beaks with giant pouches of soft, elastic skin, which they use to scoop up fish from water. The pouch is so massive that it can hold several times more food than the pelican's stomach. Fully stretched underwater, it can hold about 13 litres (three gallons) of water, as much as a large bucket.

Fantastic fit

The snail kite of North and South America has a long, curved beak that fits exactly inside the shell of the apple snail on which it feeds. Its beak can cut through the muscle holding the snail in its shell.

Food and feeding

Feasting or starving

The smaller a bird is, the more time it needs to spend feeding. Big eagles can starve for several days without ill effect, but the tiny goldcrest of Europe needs to eat all day long in winter just to have enough energy to survive the nights.

Heavy hoatzin

The odd-looking hoatzin of the Amazon forests eats leaves and fruit. Its food is stored and also partly digested in an enormous crop, which weighs about one-third of its body weight. The hoatzin is a poor flier and when its huge crop is full it even has difficulty jumping from branch to branch in the trees where it lives.

Cuckoo's caterpillars

Hairy caterpillars have a mild poison in their hairs which brings people out in a rash and makes most birds that might eat them sick. But the cuckoo is able to eat this tasty treat. Every so often, the inside of the cuckoo's stomach, including the caterpillar hairs, peels away and the cuckoo coughs it up in a ball.

Vampire bird

The sharp-beaked ground finch of the Galapagos Islands is a seed-eater, but it is also known to behave like a vampire. Using its sharp beak, it pecks holes in the wings of nesting masked boobies and drinks their blood. The boobies do not seem to mind and the finches get a nourishing drink.

Feeding in flight

Swifts are remarkable for spending virtually their whole lives in the air. They sleep, feed and drink on the wing. To feed, they open their wide mouths and catch flying insects. As a result, the swift's beak has become reduced to little more than a rim around its mouth.

How much food?

Bird	Average food per day	Equivalent to
Pelican	1.8kg fish	Half its body weight
Eagle	up to 1kg meat	Quarter of its weight
Giant hummingbird	15g nectar or insects	Over half its weight
Waxwing	210g berries	Three times its weight

Not a fussy feeder

The bird with the widest variety of diet ever recorded is the North American ruffed grouse. Its food is known to have included at least 518 kinds of animals and 414 different plants.

Woodpecker weapons

Woodpeckers have strong, pointed beaks to chisel into wood and sensitive, long tongues to probe for insects and grubs. The tongue may be sticky, as in the green woodpecker, or barbed and harpoon-like as in the great spotted woodpecker. A special mechanism allows it to extend over 10cm (4in) beyond the beak tip.

Hummingbirds

Hummingbirds feed on nectar, sucking it up with their long tubular tongues while they hover in front of flowers. Although they appear to be still while hovering, their wings beat at incredible speed with the tips tracing a figure of eight. Up to 80 wing beats per second have been recorded.

Gulls and golf balls

Gulls will pick up unopened shellfish and drop them from a height in an attempt to get at the tasty contents. Herring gulls have been known mistakenly to try this out on golf balls.

Buzz, buzz, buzzard

Although it is a very large bird, the honey buzzard feeds on wasps and bees. It follows them to their nests and then digs out the grubs and honeycomb wax. The buzzard has dense feathers on its face to protect it from stings.

Amazing But True

Bullfinches raid fruit orchards, eating flower buds on the fruit trees. No-one knows why, but they are very choosy. They will strip all the flowers off Conference pear trees but not touch some other varieties.

13

Biggest and smallest

Almighty ostrich

The African ostrich is the largest living bird. Males are larger than females and can be 2.7m (9ft) tall. They weigh up to 156kg (345lb), which is about 90,000 times heavier than the smallest hummingbird.

Group	Biggest birds	Weight
	Biggest	
Swans	Mute swan	8-12kg
Herons	Goliath heron	4.3kg
Owls	Eagle owl	4kg
Crows	Raven	1.7kg
Hummingbirds	Giant hummingbird	20g

Big babies

Some birds are at their heaviest when they are very young. A wandering albatross nestling weighs up to about 16kg (35lb). It loses a lot of this when it starts to exercise its wings and is about one third lighter by the time it is able to fly properly.

Heaviest flier

The world's heaviest flying birds are the kori bustards of eastern South Africa. Huge males weigh up to 18.1kg (40lb), which is about the same as a full-size television. They have a wingspan of 2.5m (8ft).

Whopper wingspan

The strong winds that blow over the world's southern oceans help keep giant albatrosses aloft for days on end, soaring around like gliders. The wandering albatross is the biggest with a huge wingspan of more than 3.5m (11ft). A recent study showed it could fly up to 960km (600 miles) a day.

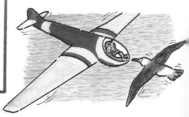

Walking on stilts

The black-winged stilt of southern Europe, Asia and central Africa has the longest legs compared to its body of any bird. In terms of size, it is rather like a slim starling walking on stilts. The stilt's legs allow it to wade in water too deep for many other birds, in search of food.

Amazing But True

When ostriches are bounding along on the run, each stride they take carries them about 3.5m (11ft) forwards. Their powerful legs are by far the biggest of any bird and can be over 1.2m (4ft) long.

Smallest birds		
Group	**Smallest**	**Weight**
Hummingbirds	Bee hummingbird	1.6g
Crows	Hume's ground jay	25g
Owls	Least pygmy owl	30g
Herons	Least bittern	50g
Swans	Black-necked swan	4.5kg

DID YOU KNOW?

The smallest bird in the world is the bee hummingbird of Cuba. It measures 5.7cm (2.25in) long, of which nearly half is its beak. It is smaller than many of the butterflies in the rain forest where it lives.

Flightless midget

The Inaccessible Island rail, which lives on a remote island in the Atlantic, is the world's smallest flightless bird. It weighs only 34.7g (1.2oz), about the size of a newly hatched domestic chick, and has similar fluffy feathers.

Egg extremes

Ostriches lay the largest eggs of any living bird. They measure about 15-20cm (6-8in) in length and weigh around 1.7kg (3.7lb). The shell is so strong that it can support the weight of a 127kg (20st) man. The smallest eggs are those laid by the vervain hummingbird. They are about 1cm (0.4in) long.

Record nests

The largest nest ever recorded was built by bald eagles in Florida, USA. It measured 2.9m (9.5ft) wide and 6m (20ft) deep. It was estimated to weigh more than two tonnes, which is about the same as two army jeeps.

The smallest nests are built by hummingbirds. The bee hummingbird's is thimble-sized and the vervain hummingbird's is about the size of half a walnut shell.

Food facts

Type of bird food	Biggest bird that mainly eats that food
Seeds	Ostrich
Leaves and grass	Mute swan
Fruit	Emu
Fish	Wandering albatross
Birds	Sea eagle
Meat	Andean condor
Insects (locusts)	White stork
Worms	Curlew

Attracting a mate

Centre stage

In many grouse species males perform courtship displays at special sites called leks. Each male claims a territory there, with the most mature and strongest commanding positions in the centre where they will attract the most females. Usually about 10-15 males gather at a lek but visiting females will choose to mate only with the one or two most dominant or attractive.

Amazing But True

As many as 400 male sage grouse of North America have been known to display on a lek about the size of 24 soccer pitches. One male mated with 21 females in a morning.

Feet first

Looking rather like soldiers, blue-footed boobies display by strutting in front of each other with heads held high. The male and female both have bright blue feet which they display prominently during their courtship.

Fancy frigatebird

Some male birds have pouches on their chest or throat which they puff out in colourful displays to attract a mate. The most showy of all belongs to the male frigatebird, whose throat pouch inflates to an enormous bright red balloon.

DID YOU KNOW?

Male birds with the showiest plumage and courtship displays do not help raise their young. They may attract and mate with many females but take no part in nest building, hatching eggs or rearing the chicks. The females have dull plumage, often mottled brown, so they are camouflaged when sitting on the nest.

Dancing cranes

Pairs of cranes perform a spectacular courtship dance before mating. In Australia, the high leaps and deep bows of the athletic brolga cranes have inspired many Aboriginal dances.

Building a bower

In Australia and New Guinea the males of some species of bowerbirds build and decorate an elaborate bower to attract a mate. The satin bowerbird builds a corridor-shaped bower of twigs about 10cm (4in) wide and decorates it with blue objects such as flowers, feathers, butterfly wings and shells. It even paints the inside of the bower with blue juice from berries, using a piece of bark.

Courting grebes

Western grebes have an extraordinary and lengthy courtship dance. A pair start by facing each other on the water, then dive and reappear side by side. Rearing up on their tails with their necks held high but their heads tilted forward, they then race across the water as if on a skateboard. The courtship continues with the pair diving and surfacing with weed in their beaks. They hold this while performing a delicate dance together.

Paradise plumage

Male birds of paradise have the most fabulous feathers in brilliant colours. Some have head or tail feathers 70cm (28in) long. Others have thin tail plumes like long, curled wires. Count Raggi's bird of paradise has brilliant red, feathery plumes on his back. He hangs upside down in a tree to show himself off to best effect. Up to ten males may display in one tree.

Preening and feeding

Many birds preen each other and rub their beaks together when courting. Others use gifts of food. The male common tern is one of many birds that offers its partner food.

Courting couples

Male and female court and pair for life	Mute swan, crow, bullfinch, owls
Male and female pair up each year to breed	Storks, herons, grebes, finches
Male courts many females. Each female nests and rears her young alone	Prairie chicken, ruff, blue bird of paradise
Female courts male and lays eggs. Male is left to hatch eggs and rear young alone	Phalaropes, African jacana, dotterel

Birds' nests

Woven nests

African weaver birds make some of the most intricate nests of all. The spectacled weaver weaves a nest of strips of leaves and grass, hanging from a branch. Starting with a ring of grass, the nest is built into a ball shape, with a long, sock-like, tubular entrance hanging from one side to keep out snakes. Some weavers build entrance tunnels as long as 60cm (2ft).

DID YOU KNOW?

Birds' nest soup is made from the nests of cave swiftlets in Asia. Huge colonies of these little birds live in vast caves, making nests of saliva stuck to the roofs and walls. It takes the edible-nest swiftlet about 30 to 40 days to build its nest. Two nests are used to make one bowl of soup.

Holed-in hornbill

The red-billed hornbills of Africa make their nest in a hollow tree. They use a tactic unique to hornbills to stop snakes and monkeys stealing their eggs and chicks. With the male's help, and using mud and droppings, the female seals herself inside the nest hole. The male feeds the female through a tiny opening.

Made to measure

The European long-tailed tit makes a beautiful, dome-shaped nest of moss and lichen, lined with feathers. Up to 2,000 feathers are used in the lining. The nest is coated with lichens for camouflage and bound up with cobwebs so that it can stretch as the young birds grow inside it.

Mallee fowl mound

Mallee fowl of Australia lay their eggs in huge mounds of earth and rotting leaves built by the males. The eggs are covered over with sandy soil and kept warm by heat from the rotting vegetation, and by the sun. The male constantly tests the temperature of the mound with his beak. If it gets too hot or cold, he opens it up or piles on more leaves and soil. These compost-heap nest mounds may be up to 4.6m (15ft) in height and 10.6m (35ft) across.

Mud oven nest

Rufous ovenbirds of South America are about the size of a thrush but build a huge, round nest, about twice the size of a soccer ball. The cement-like nest is made of mud mixed with grass and hair, and may weigh up to 10kg (22lb). It has an arched entrance from which a tunnel leads to an egg chamber.

Perched on a support such as a tree stump or fence post, it looks like a native mud oven, which is how the birds got their name.

Fostering and stealing

Some birds lay their eggs in other birds' nests. Some, such as the European cuckoo, use the other, often much smaller bird as a foster parent to hatch their eggs and raise their chicks. Others, such as the American bay-winged cowbird, simply steal nests. They throw out the eggs in them, then lay their own and rear their chicks.

Amazing But True

Pied wagtails built a nest behind the radiator grille of the Royal Society for the Protection of Birds' van at Sandy, England. The van continued to be used while eggs were laid and incubated. Four young were hatched and successfully fledged.

Nesting under a roof

The nest colonies of the sociable weaver in southern Africa look like huge growths in the tops of trees. Up to 300 nest chambers may be built in one colony. The birds first lay straws across a large branch to make a roof. Straw nests are then built under it, with the straws' sharp ends facing down the entrance tunnels, making it hard for baboons to reach in or small animals to enter.

Nest materials

Bird	Nest usually made of
Swallow	mud, saliva
Toucan	wood chips, regurgitated seeds
Hummingbird	cobwebs, moss, leaves, petals
Chaffinch	moss, lichen, feathers, hair
American robin	twigs, grass, fibre, mud
Shag	twigs, seaweed
Flamingo	mud
Waxwing	twigs, grass, pine needles, lichen
American wigeon	grass, down feathers
Kingfisher	fish bones
Mute swan	reeds, bulrushes
Eared grebe	waterweeds
Penduline tit	pussy willow down, grass
Golden palm weaver	coconut palm leaf fibres

Eggs and young

Keeping eggs cool

Most eggs must be kept warm, at about 35°C, in order to hatch them. But the grey gull, which nests in the hot deserts of Chile, has to cool its eggs to keep them at the right temperature. Instead of sitting on the eggs as most birds do, it stands over them, keeping them cool in the shade of its body.

Timing it right

Blue tits lay about 12 eggs in spring. They feed their chicks on small caterpillars which hatch out to feed on new leaves just when the blue tits' eggs hatch. Because of this precise timing, blue tits have only one chance to rear chicks each year.

Little and often

Blackbirds feed their chicks on worms, which they can find all year round. They lay only four eggs, compared to the blue tit's 12, but raise an average of three broods in a season. So blackbirds can have up to 12 young, the same as blue tits, but spread them out through the summer.

Busy parent birds

Baby birds in the nest constantly demand food. A pair of great tits carried food to their chicks 10,685 times in 14 days. A female wren fed her young 1,217 times in 16 hours.

Criss cross bill

Newly hatched crossbill chicks have small, straight beaks so that their parents can feed them. After about two weeks, the upper part of the beak starts to grow and by about six weeks it bends over the lower part, forming the typical crossed bill.

Egg and chick facts

Bird	Eggs laid	Hatched after	Chicks cared for
Mallee fowl	5-35	63 days	no parent care
Mute swan	5-7	34-40 days	87 days
Emu	7-16	59-61 days	3-6 months
Wandering albatross	1	75-82 days	9-12 months
Ptarmigan	3-12	25 days	10 days
Emperor penguin	1	62-64 days	5 months
Crossbill	3-5	12-13 days	24 days
Golden-winged warbler	4-6	10-11 days	10 days

One nest of the North American redhead, a species of duck, was found to have 87 eggs. This enormous number was created by several ducks making use of the same nest, instead of each building their own. Nests where such an unmanageable number of eggs has been laid are nearly always abandoned.

Liquid diet

Newly hatched flamingo chicks have an unusual diet. They are fed on liquid produced by their parents, rather like mammals feed their young on milk. The nourishing liquid comes from the parent's crop and dribbles out of the beak as a dark, reddish colour.

Spot the chicks

Gouldian finches of tropical Australia lay their eggs in a dome-shaped, grass nest with a side entrance. Their chicks are hatched with luminous or reflective marks inside their mouths, which glow in the dark. This makes sure the parents can see them in the darkness of the nest to feed them.

Too fat to fly

Young gannets are fed so much fish that they become too fat to fly. Their parents give up feeding them when they can eat no more. They then scramble to the cliff edge and drop into the sea, where they swim off, heading south for the winter. They starve for a week or two until they are light enough to get airborne and fly the rest of their journey.

Egg recognition

No birds' eggs ever look identical. Even those in a single clutch laid by one bird will all be slightly different in colour or markings.

Guillemots lay the most varied eggs of all. They may be white, yellowish, blue or blue-green with dark lines, spots or blotches. Huge numbers lay eggs side by side on bare cliff ledges. The enormous variety helps each bird to spot its own egg when returning from a fishing trip.

DID YOU KNOW?

Baby birds have an "egg tooth" to help them break out of the shell. This is a tiny knob at the tip of the beak. Most chicks take about 30 minutes to an hour to hatch out, but chicks of large albatrosses may need six days to get out of their tough eggshell.

Sea birds

Colour-coded chicks

Kittiwakes vigorously defend their nests high up on narrow cliff ledges, chasing off any strange adult that has appeared in their absence. To make sure youngsters are not attacked by mistake, they have black on the back of their heads, which contrasts with the adults' white heads.

Porpoising penguins

Penguins are excellent swimmers. Using their wings as flippers to propel themselves along, they swim up and down through the surface of the sea like dolphins. Their top speed is about 9kph (5.5mph). They can shoot out of the water on to land or ice in one leap of up to 2m (6ft).

Foul fulmars

Fulmars belong to the group of sea birds called tube-noses, with tube-shaped nostrils on their beaks. The name fulmar may come from the word "foul", as the birds defend their nests by spitting foul-smelling oil from their stomachs at intruders.

Amazing But True

In 1979 an Aleutian tern took the wrong route and was found in England when it should have been 8,000km (5,000 miles) away in Alaska, USA. Instead of flying north to Alaska after wintering in the northern Pacific Ocean, it flew east and crossed the Atlantic Ocean.

Breeding in millions

Many sea birds find safety in numbers at breeding time. Colonies of penguins in the southern oceans contain millions of birds. Biggest of all is a colony of ten million chinstrap penguins in the South Sandwich Islands. This colony covers an area the size of 1,000 soccer pitches.

Taking the plunge

Gannets plunge-dive into the sea from heights of up to 30m (100ft) to catch fish. To help them survive the impact of the water on their bodies, they have spongy bone around the head and beak, and air sacs under the skin around the throat and breast.

Pattering petrels

Storm petrels fly low, fluttering over the sea in search of shrimps and plankton. The Wilson's storm petrel flies so close to the water its webbed feet patter along on the surface, so that it appears to be hopping or skipping along.

Penguin profiles

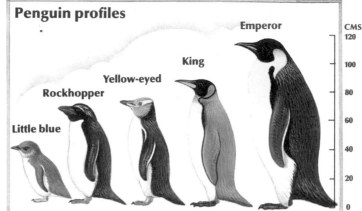

Little blue
Rockhopper
Yellow-eyed
King
Emperor

| CMS |
| 120 |
| 100 |
| 80 |
| 60 |
| 40 |
| 20 |
| 0 |

There are 18 species of penguins. All live south of the Equator, but only six live in Antarctica.

Pirates in the air

Skuas steal food from other ocean birds. The arctic skua catches fish and small birds, but is more likely to use its speed and flying skill to chase kittiwakes and terns, making them drop or cough up their food.

DID YOU KNOW?

Emperor penguins dive down to depths of 265m (870ft), staying under for up to nine minutes, occasionally even twice as long. Between dives, they comb their feathers to trap air in them, which helps to keep them warm in the cold water.

Swoop and scoop

Frigatebirds fly over the sea, often far from land, but never swim. They spend almost their whole lives in the air, using their enormously long wings and long, forked tail to fly with great agility. Like skuas, frigatebirds are pirates. They harass birds such as boobies, scooping up dropped food in the air with a swift downward swoop.

Gull facts

Largest	Great black-backed gull
Smallest	Little gull
Most common	Kittiwake
Rarest	Relict gull (in Siberia)
Hardiest	Ivory gull (lives in Arctic)
Longest-lived	Herring gull (44 years)
Largest colonies	Kittiwake

Water birds

Waders

There are about 200 species of wading birds, most of which feed in soft mud and sand at the water's edge. Different species can feed in the same place without competition as their beaks are adapted for finding different foods. Those with short beaks pick food from on or just below the surface. Those with longer beaks mainly probe deeper for worms and shellfish.

Beaks less than 5cm long – ringed plover, knot, sanderling, turnstone, dunlin

Beaks 5-10cm long – redshank, black-tailed godwit, oystercatcher, snipe, avocet

Beaks over 10cm long – curlew

Stained cranes

The adult sandhill crane of North America has grey plumage. But the feathers of its back, neck and breast often become coloured with rusty brown stains. Living by or near to marshes, it preens itself with a muddy beak in which there may be traces of iron, which causes brown staining.

Snake bird

The anhinga, or snake bird, gets its name from its long, snake-like neck and head, often the only part seen when it is swimming. It uses its sharp, pointed beak to spear fish, then tosses them into the air with a violent shake of its head, so it can catch and swallow them. Just like a snake swallowing food, its neck bulges as large fish pass down.

Skimming the water

Skimmers look as if they have upside-down beaks, as the lower part is longer than the upper. They fish in shallow water, flying with the lower part of the beak slicing through the water like a knife. When it touches a fish, the skimmer nods its head down and snaps its beak shut to catch it.

Amazing But True

Bright blue swans were seen on a river in the city of Norwich near the east coast of Britain in April 1990. A chemical is thought to have polluted the water but, luckily, the swans did not seem to suffer.

Whirlpool water bird

Phalaropes often spin around in circles while swimming. This creates a whirlpool, which stirs up the small animals on which they feed.

Diving from danger

Moorhens swim on ponds and lakes with their heads nodding vigorously. But if danger threatens, they dive underwater. They stay under by gripping weed with their feet and poke the tip of the beak above water to breathe.

Heron umbrella

To catch fish, the black heron crouches in water and holds its wings like an umbrella, shading the surface from the bright African sun. It may do this to see the fish more clearly, or the fish might be attracted to swim into the shade.

Sawbills

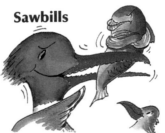

Red-breasted mergansers are sawbill ducks. They have narrow beaks with edges toothed like the blade of a saw. This gives them a firm grip on slippery fish.

DID YOU KNOW?

Bewick's swans have black and yellow faces but each one has a unique pattern. Hundreds of them arrive to winter in England from Siberia each year. Many have been given names and can be easily identified without having to be caught.

Diving dipper

The dipper is the only songbird that dives underwater to feed. It stands on rocks in streams, bobbing up and down, dipping its head into the water to look for insects, worms and snails. It uses its wings to swim underwater and can even run along on the bottom.

How ducks feed

Grazers graze on grasses and other plants on salt marshes and grassy banks.

Wigeon, American wigeon

Dabblers feed on or just under the water. They can up-end, or tip up, to reach down further.

Gadwall, pintail, mallard, shoveler, teal, black duck

Divers can dive down to the water bed. They can stay under for half a minute or more.

Pochard, goldeneye, tufted duck, eider, ring-necked duck, merganser

Birds of prey

Hunters in the sky

Birds of prey are hunters, feeding on mammals, other birds, fish, insects and snakes. Owls alone hunt by night; all the others belong to a group called raptors and hunt by day. The main features of raptors are:

Excellent eyesight
Strong, hooked beaks for tearing flesh
Large feet for holding and carrying prey
Strong, sharp, hooked claws or talons for grasping prey and killing it
Powerful wings

Fire followers

Insect-eating birds of prey such as kites follow grassland fires for an easy food supply. They feed on insects that take to the air to escape from the burning grass.

Eagle eyes

Birds of prey have the best eyesight of all birds. Golden eagles, which have eyes of a similar size to ours, can see a hare from a distance of 3.2km (2 miles) in good light against a contrasting background.

Vegetarian vulture

The palm nut vulture of West Africa is the only vegetarian bird of prey. Its main food is the fruit of the oil palm tree, which it plucks from among the dense palm fronds. It also eats shellfish and fish.

DID YOU KNOW?

Like many raptors, female sparrowhawks are much bigger than males. Males catch small birds like finches and tits, while females prey on larger birds such as thrushes and pigeons. This may help them to avoid competing for food, so larger numbers can live in one area.

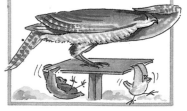

Raptor records

Biggest	Andean condor	12kg (3.1m wingspan)
Smallest	Philippine falconet	35g (150mm long)
Fastest	Peregrine falcon	about 100kph (level flight)
Rarest	Madagascar serpent eagle	probably less than 10 birds
Longest-lived	Andean condor	20-30 years average lifespan

Bone-breaker

Big birds of prey

Group	Biggest bird	Wingspan
Vultures	Andean condor	3.1m
Eagles	Wedge-tailed eagle	2.84m
Owls	Eagle owl	2m
Buzzards	Upland buzzard	1.9m
Kites	Red kite	1.8m
Harriers	Marsh harrier	1.6m
Falcons	Gyrfalcon	1.6m
Hawks	Northern goshawk	1.5m

One of the biggest vultures with a wingspan up to 3m (10ft) is the bearded vulture or lammergeier, also called the bone-breaker. It carries large bones from dead animals up to 80m (260ft), dropping them on to rocks to break them. It then eats the marrow and shattered bone. Lammergeiers also eat tortoises, using the same method to crack open their shells.

Ferociously fast

When hawks and falcons spot prey, they dive at great speed and hit it hard with outstretched talons, often killing it instantly. The peregrine falcon is one of the fastest, making spectacular, steep dives on to prey in mid-air at speeds of at least 180kph (112mph).

Late start

Eleonora's falcons breed on Mediterranean islands in the autumn, long after most birds have reared their young. The chicks are hatched to coincide with the southbound migration of millions of small birds, which make easy prey for the falcon to feed to its hungry brood.

Flexible approach

The harrier hawk has double-jointed legs, which it uses in its search for eggs or chicks in tree hole nests. It clings on to the edge of a tree hole with one foot, bending its leg backwards so it can reach its other foot down into the nest.

No monkeying around

The huge harpy eagle of the South American rain forests causes terror in the treetops. It flies skilfully among the trees at up to 80kph (50mph), snatching up monkeys and sloths.

Tropical forest birds

Parrot power

Most parrots live in pairs or noisy flocks in tropical forests. They have strong, hooked beaks, which they often use in climbing. Macaws can even hang from branches by their beaks. Parrots' feet are also powerful tools and are unique in being used like hands to hold food.

Pitta patter

Pittas are colourful, plump birds with short tails and long, strong legs. Although quite able to fly, they run around on the forest floor and fly only when necessary.

Antbirds

Swarms of soldier ants marching across the forest floors in Panama are often accompanied by antbirds. The birds rarely eat the ants, but prey on the insects that are disturbed by them.

Bee my guide

The greater honeyguide of Africa is so-called because it guides honey badgers to bees' nests. The bird will call to a honey badger, or even a human, to make it follow to where it has found a bees' nest. It waits while the badger breaks open the nest to get the honey. It can then eat the grubs and beeswax.

Hanging about

Sparrow-sized hanging parrots have an unusual form of camouflage. They hang upside down from a branch, bent double, and look just like leaves. They roost in this position and may even feed like this.

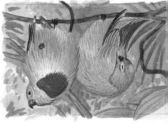

Parrot facts

Largest	Hyacinth macaw	100cm long
Smallest	Buff-faced pygmy parrot	8.4cm long
Rarest	Spix's macaw	under 10
Most widespread	Rose-ringed parakeet	Africa and India
Longest-lived	Sulphur-crested cockatoo	82 years (in captivity)
Country with most species	Australia	52 species

Top heavy toucan

Being 50cm (20in) long, the keel-billed toucan is a large bird, but much of this length is taken up by its huge, colourful beak. Although toucans' beaks look top heavy, they are actually hollow and very light. They are used to reach fruit from branches too small to bear the birds' weight, but why they are so huge and remarkably colourful is a mystery.

Aerial acrobats

No other bird beats the hummingbirds for aerial skills. As well as being able to hover in mid-air while they suck nectar from flowers, they can fly sideways, backwards, and even upside down. Their wings make a humming noise as they fly, which is how they got their name.

Birds to be wary of

Cassowaries are large, flightless birds of the rain forests of northern Australia and New Guinea. On their heads they have a horny casque, like a helmet, up to 15cm (6in) high. This protects them as they push through dense undergrowth. They defend themselves with powerful kicks, and are known to have killed humans with their dagger-like claws.

Preparing for paradise

The preparation made for courtship display by male birds of paradise is as elaborate as the display itself. In the forests of New Guinea, the magnificent bird of paradise clears an area about 6m (20ft) wide, even pulling leaves off trees to make sure of enough sunlight in which to show off his plumage.

Diet with a difference

Scarlet macaws in the mountain forests of South America gather on river banks and other earth cliffs to eat soil. They get vital minerals from the soil, which their diet of fruit and seeds lacks.

DID YOU KNOW?

Almost half the world's bird species are found in the tropical forests of South America. They are either breeding there or have travelled to escape the North American winter. But an area of rain forest about the size of six soccer pitches is being destroyed every minute. At this rate, most of the forests and their bird life will be gone in ten years' time.

Birds of grasslands . . .

Rich pickings

Vultures glide high over the African savanna for hours on end. They rarely kill prey, but fly thousands of kilometres in search of fresh carcasses. As many as 200-300 vultures may gather at a large carcass, as the birds use their keen eyesight to spot when others far away fly down to feed.

Secretary bird

The secretary bird of African grasslands is a unique bird of prey which hunts on foot. Striding about on very long legs, it hunts for small animals, including deadly poisonous snakes, which it kills by stamping on them.

Burrowing owl

The burrowing owl lives in deserted prairie dog burrows on the American plains. It hunts at night, but often stands at its burrow entrance during the day. When alarmed, it can frighten enemies by making a sound exactly like a rattlesnake.

The huge flightless emus of Australia's scrubland may roam hundreds of kilometres in a year in search of food and water. In 1932, both farmers and the Royal Australian Artillery waged war as many of the 20,000 emus on the move attacked crops. Eventually, a barrier fence 1,000km (620 miles) long was put up to protect the farms.

Amazing But True

The estimated population of the red-billed quelea of southern Africa is 100,000 million, making it the world's most numerous bird. It is also the world's worst bird pest, as flocks of at least 10,000, and sometimes millions, feed together, destroying entire crops like a swarm of locusts.

Dry grassland birds

Typical birds of dry grasslands are:
Europe – Stone-curlew
Asia – Pallas's sandgrouse
Australia – Emu
N. America – Meadowlark
S. America – Rhea
Africa
(southern) – Kori bustard
(northern) – Temminck's courser

and deserts

Thirsty work

Sandgrouse live in deserts and fly up to 80km (50 miles) to a waterhole to drink every day. Young chicks cannot fly to reach water, so parents take it to them. They ruffle their belly feathers and soak them in water, then fly back to the nest with the water held in their feathers like a sponge which the chicks can suck. Sandgrouse may carry water like this for 30km (20 miles).

Cool colours

In deserts, colour is important for camouflage and keeping cool. The most common colouring is cream, sandy or white to blend with sand or rock. Light colours reflect heat, whereas dark ones absorb it, so pale plumage also helps birds to stay cool.

Living with little water

Deserts have less than 25cm (10in) of rain a year. Birds can live where there is so little water because they lose so little from their bodies. Their urine is much more concentrated than that of mammals and they have a higher body temperature, so they lose less water by evaporation to keep cool. In some desert birds, water loss is reduced even further by their body temperature rising during the day.

Desert fortresses

Cacti are home for some desert birds. The sharp spines keep out enemies. In America, elf owls roost and nest in holes in saguaro cacti and cactus wrens build nests in among spines of the cholla cactus.

Roadrunner

The roadrunner lives in the deserts of Texas and Mexico. Although it can fly, it usually dashes around on foot, grabbing lizards and small snakes with its beak for food.

Keeping cool

Birds have various ways of coping with high desert temperatures. Some keep cool by panting, some stand with their backs to the wind to catch cooling breezes and some go

underground in abandoned burrows or stay in the shade of rocks. Long legs help birds to keep cool, as more heat is lost from bare legs than feathered bodies. The turkey vulture even squirts excrement on to its legs and feet to cool itself.

Nocturnal birds

Batty bird

The oilbird lives in dark caves in South America. It spends its whole life in darkness, only leaving the caves at night to feed on the fruits of forest trees. Amazingly, it finds its way around in the caves by echo-location, like a bat. It makes tiny, clicking sounds and uses their echoes to tell how far it is from the walls or other oilbirds.

DID YOU KNOW?

Storm petrels spend their lives far out at sea, but have to come to land to nest. They are so weak and easy for predators to catch that they only come ashore on dark nights. Each bird finds its way to its burrow by listening to the calls of its mate and by using its very good sense of smell.

Flexi-necks

Owls have such huge eyes that there is no room to move them in their sockets. Instead, they turn their whole heads to look sideways. They have very flexible necks and can turn their heads right round to look backwards and even upside down.

Green for go

The American black skimmer sometimes feeds at night. It flies over water dragging its long beak through the surface and this stirs up luminous plankton which glow green along the skimmer's trail. Fish are attracted to the green colour, and the skimmer flies back along the same line to snatch them up.

Ear, here!

Owls' hearing is superb. Many have feathery tufts that look like ears, but in fact, their ears are large openings hidden just behind the flat discs of feathers around their eyes. The discs probably help to direct sounds into their ears. In many owls one ear is bigger than the other and one is often higher than the other. This difference makes it easier for an owl to judge exactly where a sound is coming from and so pinpoint its prey even in pitch darkness.

Sense of smell

Kiwis are unique in having nostrils at the tip of their long beaks. Most birds have nostrils at the base of the beak and use hearing and sight rather than smell to find food. But kiwis are nocturnal birds and use their sense of smell to find earthworms and insects in the dark.

Night activity

The main reasons for nocturnal activity are:
Less competition for food
Access to food not available in the day
Safety from predators for feeding or breeding

Amazing But True

The little blue or fairy penguin of southern Australia is shy at sea and nocturnal on land. But despite this, it has accustomed itself to the glare of publicity and floodlights on Phillip Island near Melbourne, the one place where it can be seen close to. Here, after dark in the breeding season, crowds gather to watch the evening parade of fairy penguins waddling hurriedly ashore to their nest burrows.

Nocturnal gull

The distinctive looking swallow-tailed gull of the Galapagos Islands is the only known nocturnal gull. Its huge eyes, for seeing squid which it catches at night, are made even more striking by crimson eyelids.

Silent flight

Unlike most other birds of prey, many owls hunt at night. To help keep their movements quiet as they swoop on to prey, their wing feathers have soft, fringed edges and they have feathers on their legs and feet.

Owl facts

Biggest	Eagle owl	71cm long (wingspan 1.5m)
Smallest	Elf owl, least pygmy owl, long -whiskered owlet	all 130cm long
Rarest	Laughing owl	probably under 10
Most widespread	Barn owl	
Strangest food	Blakiston's fish owl	crayfish
Noisiest	Pel's fishing owl	voice carries 3km
Longest-lived	Eagle owl	72 years (in captivity)

Bird voices

Variety of voices

Birds use their voices to communicate in calls and songs. Calls are simple notes, often not musical, used for a warning and to keep contact within a group. Songs are used to attract a mate and to advertise the ownership of territory. Some birds' voices have been given special names:

Bittern	boom
Diver	wail
Grebe	whinny
Oystercatcher	pipe
Nightjar	churr
Mallard (duck)	quack
Goose	honk
Owl	hoot
Dove	coo
Swift	screech

Name that tune

Many birds are named after their calls. The chiffchaff, cuckoo, curlew, kittiwake, chickadee and towhee all call their name. Some American nightjars make sounds like their names: the whip-poor-will, the poor-will and the chuck-wills-widow.

Blooming booming

In New Zealand, male kakapos make a loud booming noise to attract females, but many years they do not boom and the birds do not breed. They start to boom and nest when there is a sudden abundance of pollen on the plants that produce their favourite fruits. This tells them that there will be plenty of fruit on which to feed their chicks.

Two tunes together

A few birds, including the reed warbler, can sing two notes at the same time and so sing two tunes at once. The North American brown thrasher even manages to sing four different notes together at one point in its song. The colourful gouldian finch of Australia is equally amazing. It makes a droning sound like bagpipes while singing two songs at once.

Different dialects

Young chaffinches can sing a basic song. But they only learn a proper chaffinch song as they grow up and hear other chaffinches singing. Because they copy each other, chaffinches in any one part of Europe all sound the same, but if birds from different areas are compared, dialects or variations can be detected.

My word!

The African grey parrot is one of the most talkative cagebirds. A female called Prudle won the "Best talking parrot-like bird" title at the National Cage and Aviary Bird Show in London for 12 years from 1965-76. She could say almost 800 words, and retired unbeaten.

Birds do most of their singing at dawn and dusk, but the red-eyed vireo, a small American bird like a warbler, sings all day long throughout the summer. One individual was once counted singing 22,197 times in ten hours.

Copycat birds

Marsh warblers nest in Europe but winter in Africa. They are superb mimics and can copy 60 or more bird voices. Scientists know where the birds have spent the winter because they can recognize the sounds of African birds in the marsh warblers' songs.

Barbet duet

Black-collared barbets in Africa make very loud, distinctive calls. But what sounds like a simple song is actually a duet. The first part of the call, "to", is made by one bird and the second part, "puddely", is made by its mate.

Contact calls

Migrating geese make loud, honking noises, called contact calls, to help them stay together.

DID YOU KNOW?

The familiar call of the cuckoo in Europe is made only by the male bird. Although paintings of cuckoos often show them with beaks wide open, they sing "cu-coo" with the beak closed.

Record voices

The Indian peacock has one of the loudest, most far-carrying calls which echoes for kilometres. In contrast, the notes of treecreepers are so high and hiss-like that we can hardly hear them.

A flock of long-tailed tits feeding in a wood constantly twitter to each other to keep in contact.

Instinct and learning

Bird brain or computer

Birds have very small brains compared to humans, so their ability to learn is limited. But they are born with an inbuilt ability to do many things, rather like a computer that has been programmed. This inbuilt behaviour is what we call instinct.

Nesting instinct

African weaver birds do not learn from one another how to build their intricate ball or sock-shaped nests, they instinctively know how. Scientists reared four generations of weavers in captivity without giving them any nest materials. They then gave materials to great-great-grandchildren of the original weavers and the birds built a perfect nest despite never having seen one.

Doorstep diet

Blue tits were first recorded pecking at the tops of bottles of milk on doorsteps about 70 years ago. From being inquisitive, tits learned that this was an easy source of food. The behaviour soon spread. Chaffinches, robins and song thrushes are among birds that have learnt to copy this habit.

Starlings on course

In an experiment on migration, starlings were caught as they flew across the Netherlands. They were ringed and released in Switzerland. southern France, Spain and Portugal. They had instinctively flown south-west, making no allowance for having started further south

Of those recaptured later, most adults were found at their usual winter quarters near the English Channel, but the young were found in than normal. Incredibly, after returning to their breeding grounds, when autumn came again they flew back to south-west Europe for the winter.

Migration mystery

Many birds migrate over vast distances, returning to the same sites year after year. Birds are known to navigate by recognizing landmarks and by using smell and sound. They also instinctively use the sun or stars as a compass. Several species are known to have a sort of compass in their heads. But exactly how all this is used to find their way is a mystery.

Telling the time

Like many other animals, birds have an accurate sense of time. If food is put out on a bird table at the same time each day, birds quickly learn to appear at that time. This sense of time tells them when to breed and when to migrate.

DID YOU KNOW?

Birds bathe in water or dust to help keep clean and get relief from irritating fleas and lice. Many songbirds have learnt to use ants to control lice. Formic acid from the ants is thought to kill the pests. Some birds stand on an ants' nest and fluff out their feathers so the ants run over them. Crows and jays actually hold ants in their beaks and rub them on their feathers. Crows even pick up twigs from bonfires or glowing cigarette stubs and use them in the same way.

Sophisticated fishing

Just like fishermen, the American green heron has learnt to use bait to catch fish. It picks an insect up and drops it into the water. If the bait starts to float away without luring a fish, the heron will retrieve it and even take it to a different place to try again.

Using tools

More than 30 species of birds use tools to help them get food or build nests. The woodpecker finch of the Galapagos Islands uses a cactus spine to probe into holes in wood and hook out grubs. It may use a broken spine or snap one off a cactus. It may even trim a spine to a more manageable length.

Relationships

Pecking order

Most birds live fairly solitary lives, perhaps joining up in groups to breed or to roost at night. Other birds live in a permanent flock. They have a strict "pecking order" and are ranked according to their aggressiveness. This establishes the birds' relationships to one another, so they do not fight constantly.

Easy pickings

Some birds use animals or larger birds to help them find food. African carmine bee-eaters perch on kori bustards to catch flies that flit up out of the way of the bustards' feet. North American cowbirds run among cattle to catch insects that are flushed out as the cattle graze.

Peregrine protection

Red-breasted geese nest close to peregrines in the Arctic. This strange attraction to the fierce falcons helps to protect their young. Goslings are easy prey for arctic foxes, but when the peregrines are about, the foxes stay away.

DID YOU KNOW?

Many parent birds use other birds without young to help feed their chicks. The helper may be unrelated, but is often a brother or sister of the parent, or older offspring of the pair. Red-throated bee-eaters often use helpers, which gives the young 80 per cent more chance of being reared. If helpers nest the next year, they may in turn be helped by the young they looked after.

Roosting

Birds gather for the night in huge roosts. A roost keeps them warmer, gives protection from predators, although those at the edges are vulnerable, and may help in finding food the next day. Starling roosts can contain a million or more birds, which split into much smaller flocks for feeding. A flock that has not found much to eat one day may follow one that fed well when they set out from the roost next morning.

Hoping for hornweed

Gadwalls are surface-feeding ducks. They like to eat American hornweed but cannot dive to get it. Instead they wait for coots to bring up beakfuls and then steal some or pick up dropped scraps.

Feeding together

Some birds get food by working in groups. Up to 40 white pelicans close in on a shoal of fish by forming a horseshoe around it, then dip their heads underwater together for an easy catch. Some cormorants swim in groups called rafts, diving together to catch fish in shoals.

Biggest flocks

Passenger pigeon (extinct)	2,230,272,000
Brambling	70,000,000
Red-billed quelea	32,000,000
Sooty tern	20,000,000
Adélie penguin	2,000,000
Starling	2,000,000
Red-winged blackbird	1,000,000
Budgerigar	1,000,000
Lesser flamingo	1,000,000

It takes two

The turkey vulture uses its good sense of smell to detect dead animals as it flies over rain forest. But its beak is too weak to rip tough hide. The king vulture cannot smell a carcass, but has a strong beak. It follows the turkey vulture, rips the hide and both get a meal.

Amazing But True

A male pied flycatcher will often try to pair with two females, but keeps them up to 2km (1.2 miles) apart so neither finds out about the other. If both the females lay eggs and hatch them out, the male deserts one and only feeds the chicks of the other.

Less of a look-out

Birds feeding in flocks spend less time on the look-out for predators and so have more time to feed. An ostrich feeding alone spends 35 per cent of its time looking around, but if two feed together, each wastes only 21 per cent of its time and so can spend more time feeding. Four ostriches in a group feed for 85 per cent of their time.

Chicks in a crèche

Some birds use crèches to protect chicks from predators. When eider ducklings hatch, they gather in huge crèches of 100 or more and are guarded by unrelated "aunty" eiders. This gives them much greater protection from gulls.

Birds in danger

Harming our habitats

In the past ten years, the number of threatened bird species in the world has risen sharply from 290 to 1,029. A threatened species is one in danger of dying out, or becoming extinct. Much of the increase is the result of our misuse of our environment, poisoning and destroying birds' habitats and food.

Water catastrophe

The Coto Doñana National Park in Spain is home to 125,000 geese, 10,000 flamingos and thousands of other water birds that rely on its marshland. Tourist hotels and golf courses built beside the marsh use four billion litres (880 million gallons) of water a year. Now, new developments threaten to take more than twice as much water again – a catastrophe for the birds.

Amazing But True

In 1979, the Chatham Island black robin was almost extinct, with only five birds left. A unique experiment by the New Zealand Wildlife Service, using local tom tits to foster chicks, brought the numbers over 100 in under ten years. Incredibly, every living bird is descended from a single female who lived to about 14, more than twice the normal age.

Birds as prey

Birds trapped and shot:
T Thrushes D Doves
W Warblers R Robins
L Larks P Birds of Prey

TDL France

TLP

TDRW Spain

TD Italy

LP Sardinia

Malta

DWP Greece

DLP Cyprus

Threatened birds are usually protected by law. Sadly, this does not always help them. A report in 1990 by the British-based Royal Society for the Protection of Birds claimed that millions of protected birds are being killed in Europe. Buzzards, goshawks, falcons and other birds of prey are being shot. Many other species are being trapped to sell as cagebirds or for food.

Captive breeding

Many species survive because they are bred in captivity and released back into the wild. Zoos are being asked to breed birds such as the snowy white Bali starling, which poachers have reduced to a population of 30 in its natural habitat in Indonesia.

Rare parrot

The New Zealand kakapo is a huge nocturnal parrot, too heavy to fly. Sadly, it proved easy prey for cats and rats introduced from Europe. Now, with only 43 birds left, efforts are being made to get some to breed on a cat-free island. Kakapos breed slowly, about every four years, but in 1990 one laid an egg, giving biologists hope.

Saltmarsh sparrow

Until May 1987, when the last one known died, the dusky seaside sparrow was the world's rarest bird. Its only habitat seems to have been saltmarsh in Florida, USA. Work on reclaiming part of the coast changed this marshland and contributed to the sparrow's extinction.

Some endangered birds

Imperial woodpecker	Mexico	extinct?
Paradise parrot	Australia	extinct?
Ivory-billed woodpecker	Cuba	under 10?
Bachman's warbler	Cuba	under 10?
Echo parakeet	Mauritius	under 20
Eskimo curlew	N. America	under 30?
Mauritius kestrel	Mauritius	under 30
Japanese crested ibis	China	about 40
California condor	N. America	40
Slender-billed curlew	Asia	under 100?

DID YOU KNOW?

The widespread house sparrow was at one time protected by law. It was deliberately introduced to other continents from Europe. But its spread was too successful. It bred so rapidly that by the time the law was withdrawn it had already become a pest.

Walls of death

Hundreds of thousands of birds are killed every year by fishing fleets. In the Pacific, nets up to 80km (50 miles) long, called "walls of death", are used to catch fish. They also kill shearwaters and albatrosses, which dive for food and get entangled. Similar nets in the Barents Sea kill 800,000 birds a year.

Oil pollution

Oil pollution kills huge numbers of sea birds, especially guillemots. Laws exist to stop ships deliberately pouring oil into the sea, but accidents still happen. In 1989, a huge spill from the Exxon Valdez tanker oiled 1,600km (1,000 miles) of Alaskan coast. Over 300,000 sea birds died, a record for an oil spill. 144 bald eagles and 1,016 sea otters were also killed.

Bird lifespans
Larger for longer

The larger a bird is, the longer it may live. But most birds in the wild do not die of old age, they fall victim to natural or man-made hazards. Lifespans of birds in the wild are difficult to study, but records are being built up by ringing birds. One of the problems is knowing a bird's age when it is first ringed.

Cocky cockatoo

The oldest known captive bird was a greater sulphur-crested cockatoo called Cocky, which died at London Zoo in October 1982. He was known to be over 80 years old and probably at least 82.

Albatross ages

Albatrosses are thought to be the longest-lived birds and the wandering albatross may live for about 80 years. A female royal albatross at Otago, New Zealand has been known for over 58 years and was already an adult when first ringed. As it takes 319 days to raise a single albatross chick and few survive long enough to breed, albatrosses need to live a very long time to make sure that enough chicks survive to replace them when they die.

DID YOU KNOW?

About 75 per cent of all wild birds die before they are six months old. Millions are killed by cats and a similar number by cars. Many more die from disease, starvation, bad weather and other predators such as rats, foxes and birds of prey.

Condor in captivity

Kuzya, a male Andean condor in Moscow Zoo, was at least 77 when he died in 1964. He had lived outside in an aviary at the zoo ever since being taken there as an adult in 1892.

Short and sweet

Small birds generally have very short average lifespans because most die when they are still only fledglings. Once they reach adulthood, they have a better chance of survival.

Breeding balance

Most birds produce huge numbers of young, which offset the losses they suffer. Each year, about seven million pairs of blackbirds breed in Britain and between them hatch about 70 million eggs. That would make a possible total of 84 million blackbirds by the end of the year. In reality, about 70 million fledglings and adults die and the population stays about the same.

Robins' range

European robins are short-lived, with an average life expectancy of just six months. So "the robin" that seems to appear regularly in a garden year after year is almost certainly a succession of different birds. The greatest age so far recorded for a robin in the wild is 12 years and 11 months, but this is exceptional.

Bird strikes

Some birds meet an early death when they are in collision with aeroplanes. Such accidents, known as bird strikes, cause major damage and expense to airlines and have also caused human deaths. Gulls are most often involved in bird strikes but pigeons, starlings, lapwings, cowbirds, swallows, martins, swifts and swans have all been identified.

Bird lifespans

	Average	Maximum known
Blue tit	1 year	12 years
Starling	Up to 1½ years	21 years
House sparrow	1½ years	12 years
Robin	1½ years	12 years
Great tit	1½ years	9½ years
Bee hummingbird	Up to 2 years	?
Kestrel	2 years	15 years
Woodpigeon	2½ years	16 years
Blackbird	2½ years	14½ years
Little owl	2½ years	10 years
Mute swan	3 years	21 years
Tawny owl	3¼ years	20½ years
Swift	8 years	16 years
Kiwi	10 years?	?
Emperor penguin	20 years	?
Common crane	?	50 years
Ostrich	30-40 years	68 years

Migration map

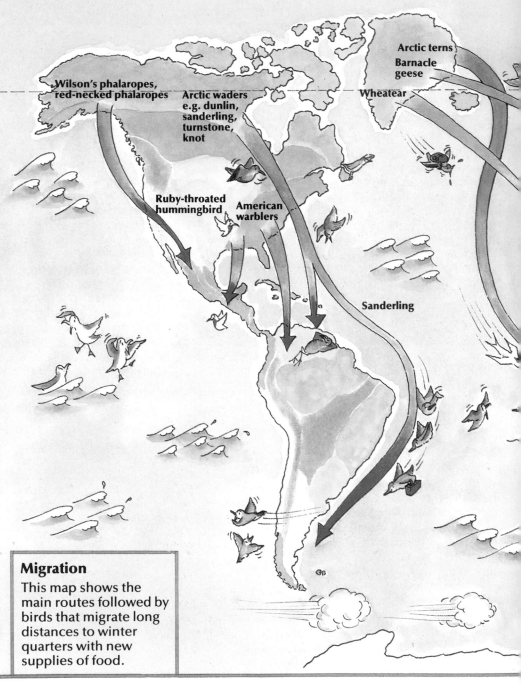

Arctic terns
Barnacle geese

Wilson's phalaropes, red-necked phalaropes

Arctic waders e.g. dunlin, sanderling, turnstone, knot

Wheatear

Ruby-throated hummingbird

American warblers

Sanderling

Migration

This map shows the main routes followed by birds that migrate long distances to winter quarters with new supplies of food.

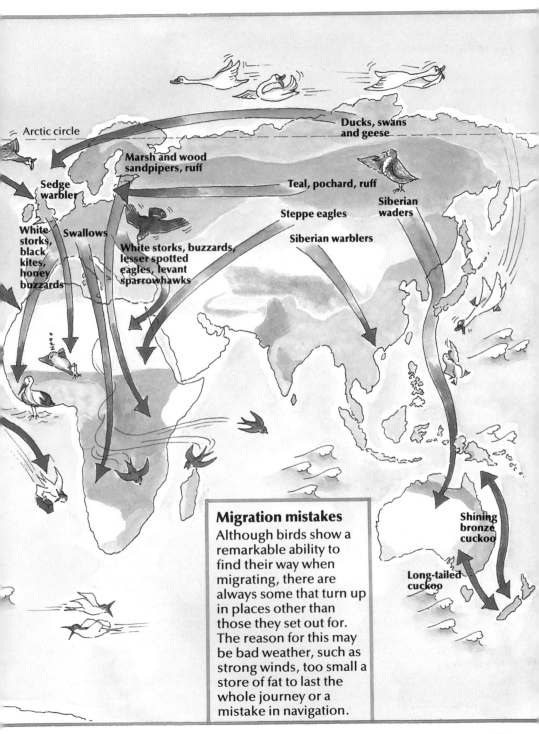

Arctic circle

Ducks, swans and geese

Marsh and wood sandpipers, ruff

Sedge warbler

Teal, pochard, ruff

Siberian waders

White storks, black kites, honey buzzards

Swallows

Steppe eagles

Siberian warblers

White storks, buzzards, lesser spotted eagles, levant sparrowhawks

Shining bronze cuckoo

Long-tailed cuckoo

Migration mistakes

Although birds show a remarkable ability to find their way when migrating, there are always some that turn up in places other than those they set out for. The reason for this may be bad weather, such as strong winds, too small a store of fat to last the whole journey or a mistake in navigation.

Glossary

Bill Another word for beak.

Breeding plumage The plumage during the courtship and nesting season. In most species, only males develop specially coloured or shaped breeding plumage to attract a mate.

Breeding season The time of year, usually spring, when birds find a mate, build a nest and rear young.

Camouflage Plumage colours and patterns that blend with a bird's background and hide it from enemies.

Clutch The number of eggs a bird lays at one time.

Colony A group of birds of the same species nesting close together.

Courtship display Special behaviour to attract a mate. It may involve showing off breeding plumage or brightly coloured skin, special calls or dances.

Coverts The feathers covering the bases of the wing and tail feathers. The tail coverts grow long and showy in the breeding plumage of some birds.

Crepuscular birds Birds such as woodcock that are most active at dawn and dusk, when they hunt for food.

Crop A pouch-like part of the gullet of many birds in which food is stored and may be partly digested.

Diurnal birds Birds that are active during the day and sleep at night.

Fledgling A young bird that has just started to fly.

Flock A large group of birds moving around together.

Glide To fly with wings kept still and stretched out.

Incubate To keep an egg at the right temperature, usually about 35°C, for the chick to develop inside, until it is able to hatch out of the shell. Most birds sit on eggs to keep them warm.

Lek An area where male birds gather to display to females in the breeding season.

Length Birds are measured from the tip of the beak to the tip of the tail, as if laid out flat.

Migration Long-distance journeys made by some birds, according to the seasons, usually between their nesting area and wintering area.

Moulting The shedding of feathers, usually once or twice a year. In most birds, feathers drop out singly as new ones grow underneath.

Nestling A young chick in the nest, unable to fly or feed itself.

Nocturnal birds Birds such as most owls that are active at night, hunting for food.

Plumage A bird's covering of feathers.

Predator A bird or other animal that hunts and kills birds or animals for food.

Roost Sleep. The place where birds sleep is also called a roost. Some birds such as waders may gather in roosts numbering tens of thousands of birds.

Wingspan The measurement from one wing tip to the other when the wings are fully spread.

Index